Rhymes for Ranga

Published by Random House India in 2010
1

Book design: Anjora Noronha, www.studiochalk.com

Random House Publishers India Private Limited
MindMill Corporate Tower, 2nd Floor, Plot No 24A
Sector 16A, Noida 201301, UP

Random House Group Limited
20 Vauxhall Bridge Road
London SW1V 2SA
United Kingdom

978 81 8400 036 8

Printed and bound in India by Replika Press Private Limited, Kundli

Rhymes for Ranga

Freda Bedi

Illustrated by Anna Bhushan

RANDOM HOUSE INDIA

Contents

Dear Reader,

This book of poems was written more than seventy years ago by an Englishwoman called Freda for her son, Ranga. Ranga grew up in Lahore, in the heart of Punjab. He would play there in the golden mustard fields, and sometimes he and his parents would go to Kashmir in the summer and trek through the snowy Pir Panchal range. Like all children, Ranga loved nursery rhymes—but there weren't any Indian nursery rhymes in English, and he wanted poems about the things little children like him did.

So, as Ranga grew, and went on his bullock-cart rides, flew his kite, and gathered eagerly around the pigeon man, his mother began to write nursery rhymes about him. India was fighting for its independence during this time and so she also wrote about Mahatma Gandhi and India moving towards freedom and standing on her own feet again.

The India that Freda writes about may seem distant, but Ranga wasn't so different from you. He loved his pet dog and all animals, he loved hearing stories and looked forward to Diwali and all our festivals. When you read these poems, imagine another time when growing up in India was very different and still very much the same.

Bhabooji

My granny Bhabooji
Gives me toys
And she's

always got

Sweet things and sour things
Salty things and spicy things
Hot little crispy bits
For greedy little boys.

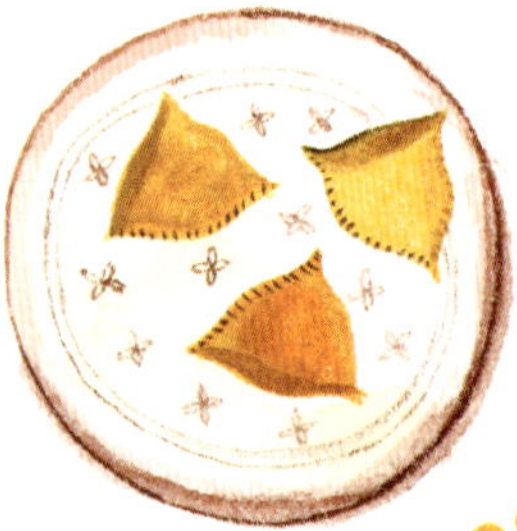

When dark growl the rain-clouds
On lumps of ice
She's

always got

Sweet little golden grapes
Mangoes of all scents and shapes
For Bhabooji's a cushion
And she feels so nice.

Bullock Cart

It's fun to play, and it's fun to swing
Or roll about in a hammock.
But I like best the bullock cart
At Dera Baba Nanak.

It rolls and jolts up to the train
To fetch our trunks and boxes.
It's really quite good exercise
For buffaloes and oxen.

Then Barkat waves his stick and shouts
For the buffaloes to start,
While I sit on a trunk behind—
O, I like the bullock cart!

Riding Round the Well

Here's a village story,
It's not so long to tell,
About a little boy
Who went riding round the well.

Riding round the well
Riding round the well,

About a little boy
Who went riding round the well.

He sat behind the buffaloes
Who work the Persian wheel,
And hit them with a stick, until
They both began to squeal.

Both began to squeal
Both began to squeal,

And hit them with a stick, until
They both began to squeal.

'What do you think you're doing?'
Said buffalo number one,
'If you hit me like that again
I'll throw you down and run.

Throw you down and run
Throw you down and run,

If you hit me like that again
I'll throw you down and run.'

'You really are a naughty boy,'
Said buffalo number two,
'If you behave so badly
We shan't look after you.

We shan't look after you
We shan't look after you,

If you behave so badly
We shan't look after you.'

'No water for the garden,
No fruit or wheat or rye,
For if we stop our journey
Well, everything will die.

Everything will die
Everything will die,

For if we stop our journey
Well, everything will die.'

'Forgive me, brother buffaloes,
I'm not so very bad.
But can't you go a little faster
Just to please a little lad.

To please a little lad
To please a little lad,

Can't you go a little faster
Just to please a little lad.'

Figures

One is a peasant,
working the plough.

Two is a milkman, milking a cow.

Three is a shopkeeper,

selling his eggs.

Four is a gentleman,
crossing his legs.

Five is a driver,
his hands on the wheel.

Six is a housewife, cooking a meal.

Seven is a teacher,
stern and tall.

Eight is a merchant,
fat as a ball.

Nine is a dhobi, with a
bundle on his head.

Ten is a thin man,
with his wife well fed.

Gulairee

Gulairee, Gulairee
Running up and down the tree
Won't you please
Come and play with me?

Some call you 'Chipmunk'
Some say 'Tree Rat'
Why must people
Call you that?

Gulairee is the name
That I like best
It suits you better
Than all the rest.

Gulairee, Gulairee
All stripey and airy
'Catch me; watch me
Gulairee, Gulairee.'

Gulairee, Gulairee
Running up and down the tree,
Even the word 'Fairy'
Rhymes with Gulairee.

Pigeons

I've got pigeons
For two rupees,
Little boy, little girl,
Buy them please.
Only
        Two
                Rupees
Buy them please.

I've got pigeons
Won't you buy?
This one circles
Up to the sky.
High
        High
                High

This one is white
And this one is brown,
And this one tumbles
Upside down.
Down
        Up
                Down
Upside down.

This one's got
An anklet as well,
All made of silver,
'Tinkle' says the bell.
Tinkle
Tinkle
Tinkle
'Tinkle' says the bell.

For two rupees,
Little boy, little girl,
Buy them please.
Only
Two
Rupees
Buy them please.

Monkey Chief

'Monkey Chief, Monkey Chief,
What do you do in the morning?'
Said the donkey with the red bridle.
'What do you do in the morning,
You naughty thief?'

'I do nothing. I swing from tree to tree.
I steal the caps of little boys.
With glee, with glee,
I play all day,' said the Monkey Chief.

'You play and swing, you wicked thief!
I am a donkey, I work as hard as anything.
I carry bricks all day.
I work hard—you only play.'

'I play all day, I am lazy and idle
But are you happy,
Little donkey with the red bridle?
The young must swing, the young must play,
It's the old who work their life away.'

Little Id Moon

Tahira, Fahmeeda,
Shameem Khatoon
All danced together for
The little Id moon.

Danced in a circle
In their little room
Danced all together for
The little Id moon.

This way
That way
Three in a line,
Three feet
Beating
All in time.

Noodles this evening
Pulao at noon
Sweet yellow rice is
For you, little moon.

Bibiji fasted
A whole month long
Now it's all over
Let's sing a song!

'O, thread of silver
Night's precious boon
Rising within us
Little Id moon!'

ABC

A B C
Wherever can you be?

D E F
Shout louder, I'm deaf

G H I
Are you in the sky?

J K L
Are you hiding in the well?

M N O
I'm hunting high and low

P Q R
I'm looking in the car.

S T U
Are you hiding in my shoe.

V and W
Ah! Now I see you.

X Y Z
Now you look for me instead.

Mummy Bird

Early every morning
When the day is new,
Sparrows fly into my hut,
One and Two.

The fat one is the father
He doesn't say a word.
The chirpy little grey one,
is a mummy bird.

They haven't any babies
I don't know why.
Perhaps they all flew up
into the sky.

Some people have babies
Five—Four—Three,
But Papa and Mama
Have only me.

So perhaps the sparrows
Haven't got one,
Poor little mummy bird
Alone in the sun.

Moti

Moti is my puppy,
He chews up everything,
Sometimes it's bones,
And sometimes it's string.

Sometimes it's shoes,
And sometimes it's bread
And often it's rice
Off my plate instead.

'Moti, do you want
To get inside my bed?'
I asked him one day,
And he nodded his head.

And now when it's night,
Very cold and very dark,
He jumps onto my cotton quilt
And he doesn't even bark.

Miss Buffalo

Miss Chambeli Clarebelle Cutty
Has eyes of blue
She lives in a personal private hutty
Does Miss Chambeli Clarebelle Cutty

Miss Chambeli Clarebelle
Won't give milk
Until she's three.
For two years more, no milk for me
from Miss Chambeli C and C.

Miss Chambeli Clarebelle
I love her dearly
And feed her well
And never will I hurt or sell
Miss Chambeli Clarebelle.

Granny's Parcel

'Ooggee, Ooggee,
Tell me please,
How will Granny's parcel
Come across the seas?'

'She'll pack it and seal it
In London Town,
And stick on the stamps
Before sundown.

The porter will load it
On the railway train
For Tilbury Dockyard
In English rain.

It will sail in the tummy
Of a huge steamship,
Past the Rock of Gibraltar
And Italy's tip.

Through the Suez Canal
And the hot Red Sea
Straight to Bombay
And to you and me.

In the fastest mail
With it's doors all shut
It will roll to the north
And into Ranga's hut.'

'O Oogee dear,
how very nice!
Will you give the postman
Annas and pice?'

The Baby Pony

Badami's like an almond
When it's roasted very brown
And Milkhi's white,
Just like the cream
We ate in Model Town.

But Chamba's just a baby
Gingery and fine,
She ought to have white stockings,
But they're dirty, just like mine.

On a slope beneath a tree
In Sawan he was born,
In front of Mali's cottage,
Near Auntie's chicken farm.

And Niru got all worried
Because his feet were wrong,
But Milkhi loved him very much,
And licked him with her tongue.

Chamba's very naughty
Always kicking high and low,
But he's only just a baby yet
And so he doesn't know.

Perhaps when he gets big enough
He'll take me for a ride
Right through the Kangra Valley
And up the mountainside.

The Kite Song

The kites sing
'Twang, Twang'.

Up in the air
By day, by night
Music comes
By the string of the kite.
Down from the sky
Not high, not loud,
Comes the song of the stars
The sigh of the cloud.

The kites fight
'Pang, Pang'.

My kitestring is covered
With broken glass,
High it is flying
None shall pass.
Strong is my enemy
Hard is the fight,
And the winner
Is my yellow kite.

Bapu Ji

In Anarkali Street
I saw a big boot
'That must be for
Gandhi's foot.'

But Mother tells me
That Gandhi's small
Just a thin little man
With no fat at all.

He's thin at the bottom
And he's thin up above,
And it's only his heart
That is big with love.

With love for India
And love for me;
To all little people
He's *'Bapu Ji'*.

'Saint' some call him
'Mahatma' too
But he's just Bapu ji
To me and you.

The Land of Nowhere

Deep in the Land of Nowhere
Before the world began
Buffaloes danced the Gidha
And stars in circles sang.

The cows wore veils for modesty
And dressed their calves in gold
And camels put on overcoats
Because they felt the cold.

Elephants wore pyjamas
And fishes walked on roads
While coolies clad in satins
Made princes carry loads.

Pigeons went a-hunting
The tail, it wagged the dog,
The lion left his kingdom
And gave it to the frog.

Goats had wings to fly with
And the donkey's tail was gone
While hens had velvet cushions
To lay their eggs upon.

Quinine was sweet as honey
And sparrows gave us milk,
Our horses sat on carpets
With turbans made of silk.

Deep in the Land of Nowhere
Before the world began
Children marked the copybooks
And teachers races ran.

The Coming of Pug and Snug

We walked along the path, through the fields and the tea
(It was Christmas time, and candles lit the tree)
And we saw a pair of Gaddi boys in caps and coats
Thick woollen homespuns, with belts of ropes,
        Bulging in front
        With a fat round lump
'What have you got there, inside the bump?'

They opened their coats, and next to their skin
Were two little heads as black as sin
Twin little Gaddi pups, born in the snows
Who their mother is, nobody knows;
        'We'll feed a pup
        On milk from a cup
Buy them, Papa, hurry, hurry up!'

'Silver for salt to savour your foods
Silver for girdles, and silver for goods
Silver for sweetmeats and silver for honey
For two little Gaddi pups, how much money?
        Rupees, one-two
        For both of you
Will you have puppies or a nice new shoe?'

'We don't want to sell them. They sleep at night
Close to our bodies and start to fight.
When morning comes they growl like bears
We don't want to sell them for years and years.
        They came the other day
        From the tents and the spray
Of the wild Gaddi torrents and the white Gaddi way.'

'In your sweet Gaddi homeland, where pierce through the snows
The curling fern fronds, the mountain rose
Where the sleek hill goats and sheep are straying
Many little Gaddi pups are rolling and playing,
        Suck milk from their mothers
        And fight with their brothers
Lots of puppies there, boys, lots of others.'

'Give us three rupees, all silver and round
Take away the puppies and keep them safe and sound.'
'I'll buy them a collar, and get them a chain
I'll build them a kennel to keep out the rain,
        One shall be Pug
        And the other Snug
And I'll roll them together in a woollen rug.'

Sherbets in Summer

Sherbets in summertime
Smelling sweet of sandalwood

Cardamom and roses
And sour yellow lime.

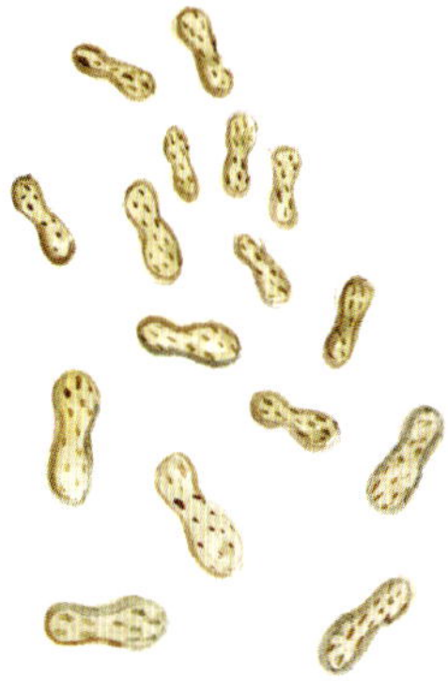

Sugar cane in winter hours
Tea made with cinnamon

Maize bread and monkey nuts
And honey from flowers.

The Old Peasant

Asks the boy

'Kisan bhai, Kisan bhai
Gold is your harvest
There's mustard
And wheat ears
Richer than a carpet.
Kisan bhai, Kisan bhai
Gold is your harvest.'

'Kisan bhai, Kisan bhai,
Your body isn't fat
And your shirt
It couldn't
Be dirtier than that.
Kisan bhai, Kisan bhai
Your body is not fat.'

'Kisan bhai, Kisan bhai,
Where is your money?
Buy me
A pony
Yellower than honey.
Kisan bhai, Kisan bhai,
Where is your money?'

Says the peasant

'It goes to the landlord
It goes to the shop
It goes to pay taxes
Drop by drop
It goes to the barber
It goes to the priest
And all that is left
Is a beggar's feast.'

Basant

Guru Nanak said to God
(white his beard as snow untrod)
'Whatever tree or fruit it yields
Does mustard grow in the Heavenly Fields?

Curd from the pitcher, well-water sweet
Out in the fields the man must eat;
Wholewheat bread and mustard grant
The heart of Punjab is the sarson plant.

Where is the winter's unsheathed lance?
Spring comes with a lyric and bhangra dance.
My daughter has yellow veils in her dower
The heart of Punjab is the sarson flower.'

'Guru Baba Nanak, look
Tender your eyes like a country brook
Whatever tree or fruit it yields:
There's a carpet of gold in the Heavenly Fields.'

And once the Buddha
walked the earth as a lion

The End of the World

There once was a hare
Who had a shady lair
And sat beneath a mango tree
When *'crash'* on his head
(So Buddha said)
Fell a *'something'* as heavy as can be.

A bump on his back
His eyes went black
And then up he jumped and started running
'For' said he
'The end of the world must be coming.'

Crying and sobbing
His cotton tail bobbing
He met on his way a timid deer,
'To see you in flight
With nothing in sight
My poor little heart is full of fear.'

'Then with me run
As quickly as you can
Because I heard a crash and started running.
Run with me, stranger,
Run, you're in danger
For the end of the world is coming.'

Came a boar and a cow
And an ox at the plough;
'Brother deer, now what's it all about?'
'You come along with us
Without any fuss
It's the end of the world without a doubt!'

And so quite soon
Like a grand typhoon
Rushed thousands and thousands of hares
Elks and hippopotamus
Tigers and rhinoceros
Boars and buffaloes in pairs.

From the jungle's depths
With lordly steps
Strode a lion to the top of the hill:
'What is the matter?
Why all this clatter?
Animals, animals, can't you be still?'

'Lord of the wood and lake
King of the forest brake
The end of the world is coming.
Helter-skelter
Let us take shelter
By leaping, and flying and running.'

'Quietly, quietly,
Calm your anxiety
O creatures of the jungle, hear my call.'
'Guide us and save us
O leader of the bravest
It's the end of the world, of us all.'

To his voice of thunder
They listened in wonder
And the lion soothed all their fears:
'Why all this panic?
Confess who began it:
O little ones, dry your tears!

Elephants, tell me.'
'Lord not we
But the hippos saw everything breaking.'
'Hippos, you?'
'Lord, not true
The tigers saw the mountains shaking!'

'Tigers, what...?'
'Lord, surely not
The rhinoceros saw it thus.'
'Rhino, rise...'
'O Lord, it is lies
'Twas the buffalo told it to us.'

'Big brother buffalo,
I want to know.'
'We don't know it, lord, for shame!
The elk folk told us
The elks made all the fuss.'
Said the elks, *'Those boars are to blame.'*

Boars rough and tusky
Voices loud and husky
Grunted with fright and with fear!
'Stories and fibs
A hit in the ribs
It came from the mouth of the deer.'

The deer sighed sadly
'Don't take it badly,
That little hare who sits so still
Told us the tale
And our hearts began to fail
And we ran like a torrent down the hill.'

'Lordly lion, spare
A little brown hare
I, I, heard the earth, you see
I heard it breaking
I felt it quaking
Right under the mango tree.'

Then spoke the lion
'Fear not, little one,
Ride on my back and come with me.
Hide not your face
Now show me the place,'
And together they hurried to the tree.

There on the ground
Golden and round
Lay a mango, flushed with red:
'Little one, a bubble
Was your silly little trouble,
It was a mango that fell on your head!

Listen, sons and daughters,
On land and on the waters
See how timid hearts go far astray,
A mango that fell
Led to panic and to hell.
Go happy to your homes. Don't run away.'

Jungle

In the jungle there are tigers
In the jungle there are deer
Two horns
Branching into twelve horns
Ba-ra-Sing-ha
Ba-ra-Sing-ha
Twelve-horned deer.

In the jungle there are leopards
Black and spotted leopards
Sure afoot
Near the torrent swift afoot
Chee-tah
Chee-tah
Dappled like the pine woods.

In the jungle there are tigers
In the jungle there are bears
Black-skinned
Brown furry mountain bears
Bha-loo
Bha-loo
Eating all the maize cobs
Sucking all the honeycombs.

Catch him, the rascal
Sell him to the jugglers
Send him to the Punjab
Show him at the fairs.

Eating up the maize crop
Black bear, brown bear,
Strike the drums of warning
Guard the field till morning
Catch him, the robber,
Dance him at the fair.

India is a Garden

India is a garden
But they took her flowers away,
They made of her a desert,
O what is she today?

India was a golden bird
They plucked her down away,
They ate her like a vulture,
O where is she today?

India is my darling
India is my bride,
I'll buy for her new ornaments
A horse for her to ride.

I'll fight for her, I'll die for her
I'll build her home again,
I'll clothe her naked children
And fill her barns with grain.

House

O I will build a house, a house
Right on top of a hill,
Where the four winds of the world
May blow into and fill.

Wind of the North
Wind of the South
Close my eyelids
Close my mouth.

Wind of the East
Wind of the West
Lay me down
And give me rest.

The night will come to my house
Built on top of the hill,
And dark will be the lake below
When the winds are still.

Diwali

Every ledge is a stream of light
And every hut a star:
India is a Milky Way
From Comorin to Himalaya.

The flowers were dead in my garden
Dead when the evening came
But from my bowls of sarson oil
Burst blossoms of flame.

The flames of the stars are silver
The light of the snows is cold
But the flame from my little earthen lamps
Is yellow as gold.

Every ledge is a stream of light
And every hut a star:
India is a Milky Way
From Comorin to Himalaya.

Mariam's Song

'We must look after Baby Jesus very carefully'
Mary said to Joseph.

Baby son
On your bed of hay
Dream the hours
Of night away.

Bullock and cow
Your playmates are;
Above you watches
The shepherd's star.

Three wise men
Are come from the East
Gifts they bear
For a baby's feast.

Gold and sandal
And mangoes sweet.
Sleep, my prince
With the lotus feet.

Incense sticks
For the messenger:
Sleep, for Indian
Nights are fair.

Bitter neem
Means sorrow to be:
Rest, my little one,
Peacefully.

Baby son
On your bed of hay
Dream the hours
Of night away.

Note: Mariam is the Indian name for Mary.

Kashmir Birthday

For planting rice
The time has come,
Another year
Has just begun.

The blossom is ended
The cherries are red.
Red is the fruit
In the strawberry bed.

Lotus crystals
On the Dal;
'The rose is pink'
Says the water girl.

White on the mountains
The snows are fair
Jewel-blue
The kingfisher.

Wagtail and nightingale
Haunt the pool:
'I'm a joker
You're a fool.'

Among the grasses
Buttercup, clover:
Summer is coming
Spring is over.

Acacia blossoms
Are flakes of snow;
The Spring is going—
Go, go, go.

For planting rice
It's time again.
How old are you?
Now I'm ten.

Mother India

She walks along with the village path
She walks along the street
With earthen pitchers on her head
And bangles on her feet.
And always little footsteps
Are following her own
And little ones are crying
Or welcoming her home.

She is Mother India
The real one that we know—
Giving all her blood and sweat
For love and not for show
Her face is lit by household fires
Worn by the earth her palms.
Mother, Mother India
With babies in her arms!

The Dawn of Freedom, 1942

'Mother, see how the bird flies
Joyful, full of song.
I want to be like that, Mother,
How long will it be, how long?'

'Son, as the river is flowing
From the mountain to the sea,
As to his hive, unthinking,
Travels the honeybee.'

'So India is marching
Straight to her Freedom Day,
And nobody shall stop her
And nothing shall bar the way.'

'And you shall be free as the bird is
Free as the air, my son!
The bars of your cage will be broken,
Your journey just begun.'

Tricolour

India's flag
Has colours three,
Fly, my Tricolour,
Over the Free!

White is our banner as mountain snow,
White as the cotton the villagers grow.

Born of the crocus its saffron dye
Rich as the mango fruit, says I,

Green its bank like the jungle's eyes
Green as the colour of sprouting rice.

Chakra, the wheel of King Ashok,
Brings peace, brings plenty, to our folk.

India's flag
Has colours three,
Fly, my Tricolour,
Over the Free.

Morning Song

The dark of the dawn
The voice of the birds
They sing a song
And these are the words:

'My child, my pelting,
The morning is coming
You cannot see it.'

The strings of the water
The flutes of the birds
Secret their music
Older than words:

'In darkness, my loved one,
The day begins
You do not know it
You do not know it.'

And the Buddha walked the earth as a deer

The Ballad of the Golden Deer

Ageless ages
Before History
In Kashi Woods
A deer roamed free.

Golden the skin
Of the Holy One
Silver his horns
In the light of the moon.

(Gentle as dew
He looked on me
His eyes beyond thoughts
And memory).

O dark the woods
And dark the sun,
To kill the deer
The courtiers came.

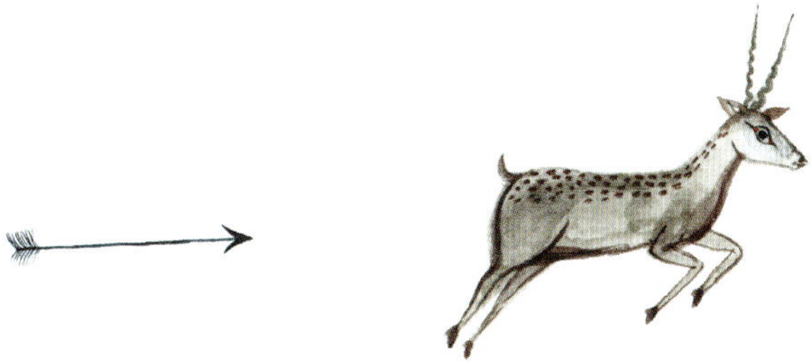

Daily they shot,
All huntsmen skilled;
Daily their arrows
The wild ones killed.

Until one morning
In heart's despair
Ran to the King
The Golden Deer.

'Take every day
One deer at least
For the butcher's knife
And the royal feast.

But let one come
Unasked, uncalled;
Let not the hunters
Ravage us all.

A hundred times
We wounded lie
Heaving our flanks
In agony;

Rather should one
In daily rite
Offer his body
In sacrifice.'

'Be it so',
The King replied,
And from that day
The wild deer died,

And willing place
Each morn their brows
On the marble steps
Of the royal house.

But in one dawn
When the sky was blood
Went the golden one
To be royal Food.

He laid his head
On the marble stone
(Whiter than milk
The holy one).

And gave his neck
To the greedy knife;
'Butcher, O butcher,
Take my life.'

'Take your life,
O Golden One?'
And the tears fell
From his eyes like rain.

'King of Benares
I know not why
But the Golden Deer
Is come to die.'

'Blessed of the forest
Why came you here?
No man may kill
The King of the Deer.'

'But today was the turn
Of a doe mother
Who suckled a fawn,
And I die for her.

She kissed my feet
And her eyes of silk
Begged for the kid
That sucks her milk.

‘Need I go
Today’, said she
‘The little one cries
So pitifully.’

And so I sped
Through the fragrant wood.
Take my life
It is meet and good.

For every day
Must the King be fed’
(Drop of blood
Are garnet red).

‘My heart is melted
O Noble One
Haste to the forest
Untouched of man.’

‘I will not move’
Said the King of the Deer
‘Until every fish
Each fowl of the air,

Each deer that hides
In the woods and sorrows
Is safe from the knife
And the hunter’s arrows.’

Then to the eyes
Of the King there came
Tears of pity
And tears of shame.

'None shall kill
And none shall harm
The forest creatures
O Gentle One.'

(Lotus hear
So late to bloom
Open your petals
Towards the sun).

Pir Panchal

Ranga, when
He was very small
Crossed the range
Of the Pir Panchal.

A meadow of snow
With never a pine
Ranga crossed
Before he was nine.

'Hold the reins carefully
The footpath is steep,
The feet of the horse
Are sinking deep.'

Warm in a blanket
Ranga's curls;
It's very cold
On top of the world.

'Icy
Chippety
Warily go,
Beneath the snow field
Waters flow.'

Safe goes the nomad,
Heart without fear,
For this is the range
In charge of the Pir.

He comes in dream
In the silent night.
His horse is blue,
And his beard is white.

'To cross the pass
The time is meet;
Sure is my blessing
For wandering feet.'

The night draws its curtains
The ponies are fed,
For all tired travellers
Food and bed.

Dear Ranga,

These rhymes grew up with you, Ranga, and they grew out of you, because it was sometimes the little words you said, and the nonsense songs you sang, that quickened something in me and gave them birth.

The first ones came when you were very small, when letters and figures were strange, fresh things. But when your sturdy baby legs became longer and thinner and school days arrived, they talked of other and more serious matters. So, side by side with the tiny poems, you could recite longer ones, too. You were walking up to the bigger world, to India, which is your country.

You wanted to know the whys and becauses of what people did. The very joy of spring-green life around you tumbled into words. So your rhymes became songs of the seasons and the festivals, of the villages, of the plains, and the hills. They were all part of you. For we don't shut ourselves up in a corner, and we celebrate all kinds of things—Id and Diwali, kite-flying and fireworks, Christmas and Independence Day.

They are yours, these rhymes, but now they will fly into print, and others will take them, too. I hope they will love them as we did, these little ones who, like you, know the English tongue, whose home is India.

Love, Mummy

A note on the author

Freda Bedi was born in Derbyshire, England and met her husband Baba Bedi at the University of Oxford in 1931. Her eldest son Ranga, for whom these poems were written, was born in Berlin, Germany and six months later, in 1934, the family came home to India. Freda took active part in India's freedom movement and was the first British woman to serve a six-month internment in Lahore jail in 1943. She remained in India all her life, and went on to work with Tibetan refugees in the 1960s, and converted to Buddhism. In 1965, Freda became the first European woman to be ordained as a Tibetan Buddhist nun. She died in 1977.

A note on the illustrator

Anna Bhushan is a London based artist, the daughter of an English mother and Indian father. She graduated from the Royal College of Art in 2004 and since then has worked on a range of illustration commissions and self-authored projects and has exhibited her paintings internationally. Anna's work is handpainted in water-colour and gouache.

www.annabhushan.com